A Little Owl Book   Holt, Rinehart and Winston, Inc., New York

Good Night, Mr. Beetle

by **LELAND B. JACOBS**

illustrated by
GILBERT RISWOLD

Copyright © 1963 by Holt, Rinehart and Winston, Inc.
Library of Congress Catalog Card Number 63-8838
Printed in the United States of America
All rights reserved.
4-9770-0813

Good
night,
Mr.
Beetle,

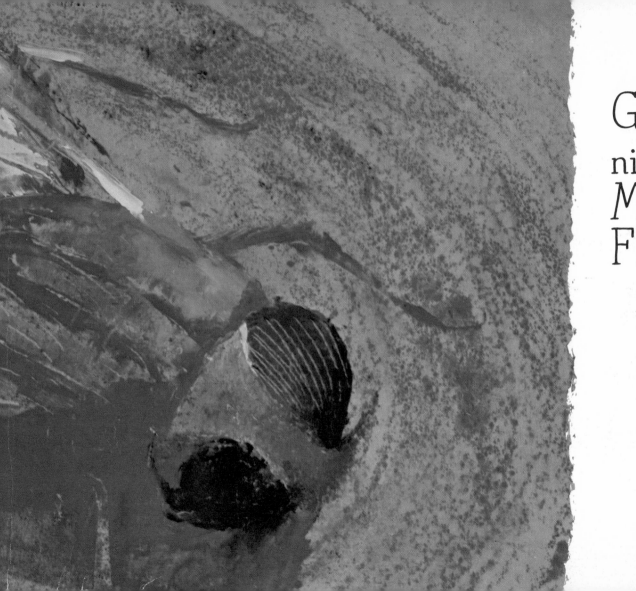

Good
night,
Mr.
Fly,

Good
night,
Mrs.
Ladybug,

The
moon's
in the
sky.

Good
night,
Mr.
Robin,

Good
night,
Mrs.
Wren,

Good
night,
Mr.
Sparrow,

It's
bed-
time
again.

Good
night,
Mr.
Rooster,

Good
night,
Mrs.
Sheep,

Good
night,
Mr.
Horse,

We
must
all go
to sleep.

Good
night,
Miss
Kitten,

Good
night,
Mr.
Pup,

I'll
see you
in the
morning

When
the sun
comes
up.